Catie & Josephine

written by
Jonathon Scott Fuqua

illustrated by
Steven Parke

Houghton Mifflin Company
Boston 2003

photography by
Steven Parke

book design & title type treatment by
Susan Mangan

story by
Steven Parke &
Jonathon Scott Fuqua

© 2003 by Jonathon Scott Fuqua and Steven Parke

www.houghtonmifflinbooks.com

The text of this book is set in FC Esprit.
The illustrations are digitally manipulated photographs.

Library of Congress Cataloging-in-Publication Data is on file.
ISBN 0-618-39403-6

Printed in Singapore
TWP 10 9 8 7 6 5 4 3 2 1

For Clay and Katy, who kept me from feeling lonely—J. S. F.

For Duncan, who inspired the idea for this book—S. P.

The Sunday morning that the Calloways moved into their new old house, Catie started looking.

She searched in every room, in closets, and even in the dusty, empty attic.

"Hello," she called. "I know you're here. I saw you run past the movers this morning. Tell me your name."

While her parents stood on the front porch, Catie sat upstairs in the hallway conducting surgery on Red Dog's torn leg. "When I was born, two of my toes were connected together by a piece of skin," she said. "Doctors got them apart when we lived in Texas, but that wasn't where we moved from. We came here from a place near Cleveland."

Later, in the bathroom, Catie opened the cabinet doors beneath the sink and whispered, "My last friend was two houses ago, when we lived in Oregon. We had an old house there, too. My parents like old places, but I don't. If we get a new one sometime, maybe we won't move anymore."

That night, as Mrs. Calloway tucked her daughter into bed, she smiled and asked, "You okay?"

"This house seems lonely."

"It won't be for long."

"All the doors squeak."

"We're going to fix them. Soon enough, it'll be our home."

"You mean like Texas and Oregon and Cleveland?"

"More than those places," Mrs. Calloway assured her. "We're going to stay in Baltimore for a while, and you're going to make friends and play and be a regular girl."

When her mother went downstairs, Catie threw back her sheets and used a flashlight to count the cracks on the ceiling. She stopped at forty, and her mind wandered back to the girl in the old dress she'd seen run through the house earlier.

Maybe instead of going upstairs, as Catie had thought, the girl had gone straight out the back door and down the steps. After school the next day, she would walk around looking for her.

2

But looking wasn't necessary.

In the early morning, before the sun came through her window, Catie heard tape being torn from a box in her room. She opened her eyes slowly, expecting to see her mother or father rooting through her things. Instead, the girl she'd seen the day before was going into her Barbie collection.

Catie said, "My mom won't let me get a Ken doll, so to make that one look like a boy, I gave her a haircut."

The girl shot a glance at Catie. "Excuse me, but I—I've got chores," she said, opening the door to Catie's room and disappearing into the hallway.

Catie jumped from her bed and chased the girl, but the upstairs was empty except for the lonely smell of burnt toast and coffee. From the stairs, she could hear her parents talking softly down in the kitchen. Nervous, she grabbed Red Dog and went to see them.

"Catieboo . . . ," her father said when she shuffled in.

"Did we wake you up?" her mother asked.

"I think I had a dream."

Her dad put down the paper. "Good or bad?"

"Kind of both. Someone was in my room."

Her mother waved her hand. "That was me. I was looking for a box I

thought might've gotten mixed with your things."

"Oh," Catie replied, absolutely sure that the person she'd seen hadn't been her mother. "Well, can I see what's on television?"

"Sweetie, it's your first day of school."

"Just for a few minutes?"

"If, while you watch, you get dressed."

"I will," she promised, but she got absorbed in cartoons and had to be reminded to get dressed.

In her old school, students teased kids they didn't like or know.

"Cynthia eats boogers."

"Neil drinks bat juice."

"Catie sucks on snails."

Catie hadn't stayed in her old school long enough for kids to stop taunting her, and she worried that, since she was the new kid, it was going to be the same way here. She'd get laughed at for five days, then it would be summertime. It was weird to begin school a week before it ended, but her parents had hoped it would help her make friends quickly.

They must have forgotten what it was like to be a kid.

After the first day in her new class, Catie drew a picture of a monster eating the school. Holding the building in one of its claws, the monster shook kids and teachers out of the windows and doors. They were all screaming, which was nice because she didn't like them anyway. She even made a person near the monster's foot look like a splatter stain.

That night, after her mother kissed her goodnight and left to unpack some more, Catie scooted out of bed and found her moonglasses, which were actually sunglasses shaped like stars. When she put them on, the room went dark. Back in bed, she pulled Red Dog close and played that she was taking a spaceship to another planet, where summer had already begun and she finally had a friend. Thinking those types of nice thoughts and still wearing her moonglasses, she fell asleep.

Hours later, Catie opened her eyes to extra, extra darkness. Through it, like a photo negative, she could see the mysterious girl moving about. Catie shifted her eyes toward the window and saw the jagged edges of her moonglasses, which, she realized, she was still wearing.

The stranger seemed to float over to wave a hand in front of Catie's face. Catie didn't move.

Seemingly confident that Catie was asleep, the girl drifted away and opened up the box with the Barbies inside. She searched about, placing the Barbie with the haircut on the floor away from her. Then she pulled out two others, one in a flowing wedding gown and the other in a hot pink cocktail dress.

"Who are you?" Catie asked softly.

The girl spun about.

Catie said, "Don't run. I just wanna know."

The girl held tight to Catie's dolls. "How can you see me? You've got blindfolds on."

Catie removed her glasses. "These aren't blindfolds."

"But they're dark."

"To keep the sun out. These are sunglasses." Catie sat up slowly. "Why were you in my bedroom this morning . . . and yesterday?"

The girl shrugged. "I'm exploring. I . . . I like your dolls. I've never seen this type before."

Catie lowered herself to the floor. She took a careful step toward the girl. "That's Fashion Barbie and that's Bride Barbie."

"I prefer Bride Barbie."

Catie asked, "What's your name?"

"Josephine."

"I'm Catie."

"I know."

Catie pointed to Fashion Barbie. "I like that one, since I don't ever want to get married to a stinky boy. I want to be a police officer. Hey, do you go to my school?"

"No."

"Do you live around here?"

"Yes."

"Well, how come you dress like such an old lady?"

Josephine smiled sadly. "My mother made me. This was her favorite dress." She took a tiny step forward. "Can I . . . might I . . . look at your toes?"

"Why?"

"Because they were connected."

"Doctors made it so you can't tell."

"Oh, well, would you mind if I ask why you have jewelry in your mouth?"

Catie touched a metal band. "This isn't jewelry. You know, these are braces. I got them so my teeth won't be crooked." She spit on a finger, reached, and pushed down a messy piece of Fashion Barbie's hair. She pressed to glue it tight, and as she worked she remembered how, two days before, she'd talked about her toes while operating on Red Dog. She said, "Josephine, you heard me say that about my webbed toes, didn't you?"

"Yes."

Down the hall, Catie's parents' bedroom door screeched open. The floorboards creaked, and a moment later her mother peeked in.

"Sweetheart?"

Catie looked at her.

"What are you doing?"

"Talking."

"With whom?"

Catie turned to point out Josephine, who she thought was hard to miss, but the girl was gone. Surprised, she glanced under her bed and behind a box, then she answered, "I'm talking to my Barbies."

"Can't sleep?"

"I guess, maybe."

That day, when Catie got home from school, her mother was painting the living room green. "It's the color of grass," Catie told her.

"Good, because they call it Grass Green," Mrs. Calloway said. "Don't you love it? I'm trying to make this house feel cheerier."

"Once I saw a girl with hair that color."

"It's better on a wall."

"Or grass," Catie said. She carried her book bag up to her room and sat in a chair. She was bored and wished Josephine was there so she'd have someone to talk to.

She got up and moved the furniture around in her dollhouse. But, since she hadn't found the dolls for it yet, it wasn't much fun. She pushed a plastic stove into a corner and said, "Josephine, instead of coming in the morning, when I don't have much time, why don't you come play now? I want you to be my friend."

Josephine didn't come, so Catie got up and drew a picture of her new school getting flattened by an avalanche. After two days of classes, the other students weren't teasing her. Instead, they completely ignored her. She sat alone at recess and ate by herself at lunch.

"Catie?"

She turned around.

Josephine stood in the doorway, her hair floating about her gently, as if in a breeze.

Catie said, "Did you hear me?"

"Hear you?"

"Did you hear me ask for you to come?"

She shook her head. "No. Did you want me to come?"

"I asked for you to."

Josephine stepped lightly into the room and looked at Catie's large plastic dollhouse. "I like that quite a lot. It's so . . . different from the ones I've seen." She slipped over and knelt down, spreading her old-style dress, with its lacy collar and rows of white, flower-shaped buttons, over her knees.

Catie sat beside her. That's when she noticed the girl's shoes, made of scuffed, old-fashioned leather. "Josephine," Catie said in a thoughtful way, "your mom makes you wear funny shoes, doesn't she?"

Josephine smiled mysteriously. "I suppose, yes."

"If you're embarrassed, I've got an extra pair of flip-flops." Catie lifted a foot to show off the purple ones she was wearing. "The ones you can wear are yellow and glow in the dark."

Josephine seemed to consider the offer before softly saying, "No, thank you." She stared at Catie. "Do you know if we're being friends?"

Catie picked a small plastic couch out of the dollhouse. "I think. But we still need to play some."

Following school the next day, while her mother applied a second coat of Grass Green paint to the living room walls, Catie hurried upstairs and called for Josephine. She kicked off her school shoes and slid into her glow-in-the-dark flip-flops. "Come on, please," she said, hoping to see her.

Josephine didn't come.

Finally, Catie quit waiting and stirred miserably through a box of toys till she found her plastic handcuffs. When her stuffed animals acted badly, she hauled them off to a jail she built by propping pillows on her bed.

From the door, Josephine said, "Good afternoon, Catie."

"You're here!"

"I saw your mother painting. She and I like bright colors."

Catie grinned. "I do, too," she said. Then she blurted out, "You know what? Since we all like bright things, maybe I should ask my mom to paint a rainbow around my whole room."

"A rainbow? That sounds wonderful."

"And—and guess what else? A humongal beanstalk could weave around it, with clouds and all. Would you like that?"

"I would." Josephine smiled. "Catie," she said, "can we play with your Barbies?"

Catie thought about it and replied, "After yesterday, I'm tired of them. How 'bout we make a show instead? I could play a princess who doesn't like strangers because I've got a solid gold goldfish that everybody wants to steal, and you could be a stranger who's playing like you're just hungry but really you're a crook."

"Can we both be princesses?"

"That—that wouldn't be as much fun." Catie looked at her handcuffs and had an idea. "Hey, let's go explore the neighborhood. Maybe we can play like we're policewomen searching for a burglar?"

Josephine's eyes drifted sideways. "I'd rather not. I don't ever . . . I can't leave my yard."

Catie studied her. "But Josephine, you had to go out of your yard to get here." She tucked a strand of hair behind an ear and stared at the girl some more. "You didn't, did you? I already figured out you live here."

"Mostly I live in the attic."

Catie leaned against the side of her bed. "Josephine," she said, "are you a fairy or something?"

"No."

"What are you?"

"I don't know."

"How come?"

"Because."

"You have to say," Catie told her.

"I remember being sick. A long time ago . . . I died."

Catie studied Josephine, then glanced at the ground. She asked softly, "How did you?"

"From the flu."

"The flu!" Catie said, surprised. "I got it twice and only stayed home from school. Nobody croaks from the flu."

"Back when I was young, back in 1918, people did."

Catie gawked at her new friend, who seemed to waver in the air like a pale, blowing cloth. "Are you a *ghost?*"

"A ghost? All I know is that I was sent back to help my parents feel better. But I think somebody forgot I was here." She lowered her head.

"You're nice, though, right?"

Josephine nodded. "I want a friend to play with. I haven't had a friend in almost fifty years."

Catie's mouth fell open. "Fifty years! That's even worse than me."

On Thursday afternoon, Mrs. Calloway worked outside trimming the wild shrubbery, while in the house Catie waited for Josephine. She unpacked her shimmeriest dress-up clothes and glimmering plastic jewelry. Catie called, "Josephine? Josephine, do you wanna look like a pop star? I even got a fake earring for you to put on your belly button. Josephine!"

After a few minutes, when Josephine didn't appear, Catie grabbed Red Dog and carefully went up the creaky steps to the attic, where she peeked around piles of old furniture that hadn't been there when she visited before. She spotted her friend reading in a stuffed chair.

"Josephine?"

The girl looked up, and for a moment her face seemed transparent before turning solid again. "Catie, you came to visit me!"

"I was calling. You didn't hear me?"

"I'm sorry. I was absorbed in this book."

"What is it?"

"The Arabian Nights."

"Oh, well . . . I got out dress-ups downstairs. You feel like being a pop star?"

Josephine said, "What's that?"

"It's a fancy girl singer who has the best clothes and dances really well."

"Um . . . maybe you'd prefer to hear a story?"

"Not so much."

"It's a really clever one."

Catie hesitated before saying, "Can I sit beside you?"

Josephine scooted over.

Catie climbed into the chair and wiggled her hips to jam in beside her friend, but unfortunately this caused Josephine to pop upward like a balloon.

Catie's eyes grew huge. "Wow. I squeezed you into the air."

"I guess you did," she said, hovering. "Sorry."

"Don't say sorry. I wish I could do that."

Josephine smiled down at Catie. "This story is 'Aladdin and the Wonderful Lamp,'" she said, and started reading about a boy named Aladdin, an evil magician trying to trick him, and a powerful genie.

While Catie listened, the scuffed floor at her feet transformed gracefully into pale sand as the roof overhead spread into an endless Arabian sky. High dunes encircled them, and camels with two humps loped past. A young, handsome man rubbed a lamp, and a genie swept from the spout.

Catie laughed. Something shiny caught her eye and she realized that her wrists were covered with beautiful bracelets and her arms were draped in exotic fabrics. It seemed so real that she felt like an Arabian princess and wished she could stay that way forever. But when the story came to an end and Aladdin became a trustworthy sultan, the desert and sky faded away and Catie was back in the crowded attic wearing her regular play clothes and glow-in-the-dark flip-flops.

Excited, Catie spun around to grin at Josephine, who was still floating. "That was *soooo* cool. It was the coolest thing I ever did."

Josephine smiled back. "What does *cool* mean?"

"It means something's really great."

"Wasn't it?"

Below them, at the bottom of the steps, Mrs. Calloway called up, "Catie, who are you talking to?"

Catie glanced wide-eyed at her friend. "I'm—I'm just playing."

"By yourself?"

"Yes."

Her mother started up the stairs.

Silently, Josephine, along with all the old furniture, disappeared.

Mrs. Calloway made a funny face when she saw Catie sitting on the dusty floor of the empty room. "Do you have an imaginary friend?"

"Do you think I do?" Catie asked.

"You were talking to somebody."

Catie looked about. She swiped up Red Dog. "I was telling him he's cool and doesn't need to go to jail."

Mrs. Calloway took off her garden gloves. "Sweetie, why are you playing in the attic?"

"Because it's big and empty."

"Why don't we go put some of your clothes away? You want to?"

"I guess."

After the last day of school, Catie sat with her mother in the kitchen. Mrs. Calloway asked, "You didn't meet any nice kids all this week?"

"No, but a mean girl named Margaret talked to me. She said her daddy is the president of a bank and can fire anybody he wants."

"That's an awful thing to talk about."

"She said her family lives in the biggest house in the neighborhood. She kind of likes my braces. She said if she gets bored with her regular friends she might have me come over to play."

"That doesn't sound very inviting."

"She's got an angry face."

Mrs. Calloway breathed out. "Catie, you know you should look at the inside of people, not the outside." She waited a moment before speaking again and the kitchen became silent. "Catie, your father and I were talking last night, and he had an idea. How would you like to go to a summer camp?"

"I wouldn't."

"There's a beautiful one in Maine where girls live in cabins and learn to make candles and weave baskets. At a camp, you could meet someone you'll be friendly with for the rest of your life."

"I don't want to go somewhere new again, and I hate camps. I heard a story about one where all the kids spit into a cup and made a boy drink it."

"You'd meet lots of girls your own age."

"I don't care."

"Catie, camps are wonderful."

Upset, Catie rose up in her chair. "Why do you and dad wanna send me away?"

"Sweetie, we'll talk about it later."

"I don't feel like talking about it!"

"Catie Calloway, sit down and don't be rude."

One day early in the summer, out in the backyard, Catie said, "Are you scared my mother might see you?"

"She can't. Grownups haven't ever seen me. That's why I haven't had a friend in so long, because only adults without kids kept living in my house."

Catie picked a dandelion and blew the fluff off. "Then, if grownups can't see you, why'd you disappear when my mom came into the attic?"

"Because I sometimes forget."

Catie wandered across the yard and stopped at the old iron fence that overlooked the alleyway. "Let's play tag or something."

Her skin faintly glowing, Josephine glided over to Catie.

"Fence is base!" Catie said, grabbing on.

Josephine lingered in the air a few feet away, and then, when she looked back at the house, Catie took off, running, jumping through the old garden, and dashing out through the fence and into the neighbor's yard.

Josephine caught up and touched her shoulder. "You're it."

Catie stopped. "It's no fair if you fly!"

Josephine floated down and ran on the ground.

Catie chased her back through the gate but quit after a couple of minutes. "We can't play tag," she said, slumping her shoulders and shuffling to the steps. "You're too quick." She sat and leaned her head against the rail.

"Sorry."

Catie said, "Josephine, I bet it's fun to be the way you are."

Josephine looked away. "It's not so fun, Catie. It's gloomy and awful if you don't have a friend."

Catie kept her head against the rail, wishing they could switch places. Then she had an idea. "Josephine, do you feel like trading clothes? I can wear your old-lady stuff and play like I'm Cinderella or something, and you can be a mean stepsister."

"Can I wear that shirt that says PRINCESS in sparkly letters?"

"I'll go get it," Catie said, and charged up the steps and into the house, her bare feet thumping loudly across the floor.

Upstairs her mother, who was cleaning the bathroom, asked, "What are you doing?"

"I'm getting stuff to play in the backyard."

"We could unpack the rest of your boxes instead."

"I don't want to," Catie told her. She slipped into her bedroom and swept up a purple plastic makeup kit and a handful of fake jewelry. She stopped at her dresser and got out her PRINCESS shirt and a pair of blue shorts covered with flowers.

Back in the hallway, she watched her mother for a second. "Do you have to put your hand in the toilet?"

"No, I have a brush for that."

"Does the brush stink?"

"I don't sniff it."

"Oh," Catie replied. "Bye!" She dashed down the stairs, through the house, and out the back door.

On the porch, Catie stopped and watched Josephine, who stood with her scuffed shoes floating above the ground, as if she had been lifted by unseen strings. She was watching a crow on a branch a few feet from her.

Catie went down the steps. "Come on, we can trade under the deck."

Alongside old cans of paint and stacks of bricks and twigs, Josephine and Catie swapped clothes. When Catie was dressed, she said, "Look at me. It's like I'm a hundred years old."

Smiling, Josephine slipped on the PRINCESS shirt and shorts. "Do I look like a regular girl?"

"Yeah. Do I look antique?"

"Yes."

Catie skipped around the yard. "Look at me! I'm old-fashioned! I'm antique!"

The back door opened and Mrs. Calloway walked onto the deck. "Catie, where in the world did you get that dress?"

Catie stopped and pinched up her mouth. "From—from Granny for my birthday."

Mrs. Calloway stared at her. "What are you doing?"

"I'm playing."

Catie's mother leaned against the porch rail. She shook her head, as if saddened by the scene. "Why don't you and I go somewhere for lunch?"

"Right now?"

"Yes, let's."

Catie looked at Josephine, who stood frozen under the porch.

"I'll go wash up," Mrs. Calloway said.

When her mother was inside, Catie hurried under the deck and whispered to Josephine, "You forgot she can't see you."

"I didn't forget. She wouldn't have seen me, but she would have seen your clothes on me."

Catie thought about what Josephine had said. She asked, "They'd look like they were on an invisible person?"

"That's how it's been. When I've worn different clothes, adults have seen them."

Catie narrowed her eyes and took off the ancient dress and put her clothes back on. "Josephine?"

"Yes?"

"You're like the neatest friend I've ever had." Catie leaped forward and hugged the girl, who smelled of mothballs and dust and felt light as air.

"You're the neatest, too," Josephine whispered.

9

For the first few weeks of summer, Catie woke up, ate honey toast for breakfast, and, as soon as she could, escaped upstairs to call for Josephine.

"Catieboooo!" her father said to her one morning, as he tried to unclog the kitchen sink.

Catie, who was rushing from the dining room, gave her empty toast plate to her mother and said, "I'm going upstairs, okay?"

Mrs. Calloway said, "Sweetie, why don't you stay down here for a while?"

"Because I really want to play with my Barbies."

Upstairs, Catie stood in the middle of her room. A few minutes passed, and she opened one of the three remaining boxes and looked inside it. "Josephine!" she called. "Josephine, do you feel like helping me unpack?"

Josephine didn't come.

"Josephine, you read too much and might get bad eyes," she said, and turned to find her father standing in the doorway.

"Catie, who are you talking to?"

"Nobody," she answered, suddenly worried about what her father would do if he found out she was friends with a dead girl.

"I heard you calling for somebody named Josephine."

"I—I made her up. I play like she's a cat that comes from—from out of a lake and has wings."

"You said she reads too much."

"That's because she can talk and read."

He studied her. "Catie, are you lonely?"

"I mostly play like Josephine and I do things together."

"Catie, we need to take a walk around the neighborhood, so that you can meet kids."

"Can we drive instead?"

"You can't make friends from a car. Plus you need to get some exercise."

"I bounce on my bed," Catie offered, and knelt down to act as if she were patting a cat. "Josephine just got here, and she's carrying a fish for us to share for breakfast."

Mr. Calloway shook his head. "A girl your age needs more than an imaginary cat for a friend," he said, and went to change for work.

That night when Mr. Calloway got home, he and Catie set out around the neighborhood. Half an hour later, Mr. Calloway's face was red with frustration. "Our real estate agent said this place was crawling with kids. I feel like she lied."

Catie said, "If you really have to know, I can tell you where a girl lives."

Her father closed his eyes. "That's a relief."

"No, it's not."

He bent down. "Why do you say that?"

"I don't like her."

"I think you're just nervous. It's tough to make new friends."

"She thinks she's important."

"I'm sure she's lovely."

"She's not."

Mr. Calloway put his hands in his pockets. "Well . . . Catieboo, if we can't find someone for you to play with this summer, camp becomes our only option. I'm sorry, but your mother and I worry you've been alone too much."

"If you send me, I'll run away."

Mr. Calloway laughed. "Of course you won't. In fact, just today I read about a camp in Minnesota that you'd absolutely love. Kids eat ice cream sundaes every night after dinner. Wouldn't that be wonderful?"

"No."

"You love ice cream."

"Not that much." Catie lifted a hand and pointed down the street. "The girl I know lives in that really humongal house. That's what she told me."

"What's her name?"

"Fat Head Margaret."

"Catie, that's incredibly rude. What's her real name?"

"Margaret. Just Margaret."

That night, when Catie sneaked up the attic steps, the attic wasn't there. The rough floor had turned into a field of soft green grass, and in the distance, a forest encircled a crumbling castle. In the middle of the field, beneath a bright blue sky, Josephine wore a beautiful princess dress and a string of pearls. She sat in the grass beside a large crow and leaned toward it dramatically. "Please, Beast," she said. "I have falleneth in love with your gentle heart and valiant—"

"Wow, Josephine," Catie interrupted.

Josephine glanced up and smiled, her skin nearly as colorless as her white dress. "I fixed the attic to resemble a picture I saw in a book. We're playing 'Beauty and the Beast.' If you would like, we can pick a fairy tale with two princesses."

Catie watched some swans fly overhead and adjusted Red Dog in her arms. She peered back at Josephine and the crow. "Is—is that your pet?"

"He's nobody's pet."

The crow turned and looked at Catie.

Josephine said, "Mr. Crow comes and visits a lot. The problem is, he hates to play make-believe. If I plead with him, like today, he will."

"Does he talk?"

"He can only talk to me."

"That's okay." Catie stepped gently onto the grass. "Josephine, I've got something to tell you."

"Yes?"

Catie stared down at her flip-flops. Tears filled her eyes. "You—you know how my dad made me look for new friends tonight? Well, we went all around and didn't find any, so he took me to visit this girl I met at school. I don't like her, but he made me go, and we knocked on the door and the first thing she whispered when her parents were talking to my dad was, 'I didn't invite you over.'"

Josephine said, "That's not nice."

"I told her, 'I came because my dad wants me to have a friend.' And she told me, 'I'm taking ballet and horseback riding this summer. I decided I don't have time to be your friend.'"

Behind Josephine, the castle vanished and the sky grew darker and darker until the rafters became visible.

Catie continued, "When she said that, I told her I didn't really wanna be her friend anyway."

Beneath Josephine, the grassy lawn faded to expose the dusty attic floor.

"Then," Catie continued, "she told me she hates my braces and that my teeth look like a giant, filthy mouse trap." Sniffling, Catie wandered over to one of the attic windows, which had just reappeared. She looked through it and down at her mother and father, who were sitting in lawn chairs, probably discussing how rude their daughter was. "So—so I yelled that she's a great big fathead who thinks she's perfect."

"Did your dad hear?"

"He heard and so did her parents. Then, when we were walking home, Dad said I have to go away to camp. That's what he told me. I gotta go away for the summer."

A breeze blew, and Josephine's princess dress transformed into the old-fashioned one she usually wore. Upset, she floated backward a few inches. "Go away?"

"'Cause he thinks I'm rude and don't have any friends."

The crow squawked miserably.

Tears streamed down Catie's face. "We just got to be friends, and you're magic and fun, and I have to leave."

Josephine didn't reply, but the entire house seemed to settle, as if it were being forced downward by a sudden shift in gravity.

Catie said, "You have to come with me."

"I . . . can't. I can't leave."

"You should try."

"But . . . this is my home."

All night there were odd noises in the attic, the sound of angry footsteps and of boxes being shoved across the floor. Uneasy, Mr. Calloway kept checking in on his daughter. "Did you hear that?" he'd ask her, and Catie always replied, "No," but she did. She heard Josephine's frustrated clomps across the wooden floor, and she heard something else that her parents didn't, her cries of sadness.

Eventually Mr. Calloway crept up the steps to the attic, and Catie heard him yelp and scamper about. "There was a crow up there," he said when he came back down. "Did you leave the window open when you were playing?"

"I think."

"Well, you shouldn't open it at all, but if you do, you need to make sure to close it next time."

In the middle of the night, Josephine, her face sickly and her cheeks ashen, floated down to Catie's room. "Everything is so terrible I can't sleep," she whispered.

Catie said, "I don't want to be by myself anymore, either. I hate it."

The following day, when Mrs. Calloway attempted to contact summer camps, the telephone line went dead, which was very strange since she'd made plenty of calls in the morning. Late in the afternoon, she quit trying the telephone and made herself coffee. While she sipped a cup, she noticed that the halls and rooms of her new old house seemed suddenly shabby and spotted with mildew after they'd recently seemed so crisp and clean. She went around opening curtains as wide as they would go, but it didn't help. That's when she decided to paint the dining room bright purple. "I want this house to feel cheerful," she explained to her family at dinner.

Later that evening the phone worked fine, but the next day it had the same annoying problem. Irritated, Mrs. Calloway banged the earpiece on the table.

Upstairs, Catie told Josephine, "She'll make my dad call from his office. We need to think of something else."

"I can't," Josephine whispered. "I'm too sad to think."

After lunch, Catie said, "Mom, what if I got a friend? Would I have to go to camp?"

"We'd consider the situation."

"Can it be a dog?"

"No."

"A cat?"

"No animals."

"It has to be a kid?"

"It has to be a kid your age."

That afternoon, Mrs. Calloway led a telephone repairman around to the alley. In the meantime, Catie sat in front of her dollhouse and settled a feather boa around her shoulders and neck. She was very determined not to go to camp. She put on her moonglasses and a brightly colored bracelet. "Josephine, do I look like a super-cool pop star?"

"I'm not familiar with what one looks like."

"I'll have to show you a magazine." Catie waited, then said, "Josephine?"

"Yes?"

"How do you make the phone disconnect?"

"I follow the phone wires to the basement and play with where they go into a box."

Catie thought about that and asked, "If you want, can you make my mom and dad see fake people the way I do?"

"No."

Catie put on three more bracelets and rattled them on her wrist. "What if I put you in a suitcase and carried you to camp? Maybe you *could* leave the yard."

"I don't think it would work."

Catie slipped on a big plastic diamond ring and studied her hand. She gazed out the window and had an idea. She spun about and said, "Josephine, what if you dress like its wintertime?"

"What do you mean?"

"What if you wear a pair of long pants and a long-sleeved shirt and—and gloves and a Halloween mask or something on your head? We could play like you're a friend from the neighborhood who likes to dress up. If my parents see I have a friend, I maybe won't have to go to camp."

Josephine blinked.

"Josephine, I have a great idea. We'll hide how you're invisible." Catie stopped. "Can you wear makeup, you think?"

Josephine stood up. "I never have!"

"What if we put makeup on your face? I bet you'd look normal."

Later, Catie swiped a bottle of her mother's skin-colored makeup and a tube of red lipstick. She went through her own drawers and boxes to find old shirts and pants that her parents wouldn't recognize right away. In the basement, she found the box of winter clothes and removed a few scarves and a pair of snow boots and ski gloves.

After hiding everything deep in a corner of her closet, Catie turned and said to Josephine, "Is the inside of your mouth invisible?" She walked over and sat in a chair next to her.

"I think it is." Josephine looked into Catie's bedroom mirror. She opened and shut her mouth. "I could keep it closed."

"Maybe, except you wouldn't be able to smile." Catie bit on a fingernail that was yellow because she'd scribbled on it with a crayon. "You think we could paint your tongue and teeth?"

"We probably shouldn't."

"Yeah." Catie thought and said, "But we have to do something."

Josephine shrugged. "I guess if we have to paint them, we should."

Catie found her poster paints and checked the colors. "The pink's all dry, but I've got red for your tongue."

At dinner that night, Catie took a big bite of a roll and began to speak. "Today I—"

"Don't talk with your mouth full," her mother instructed.

She finished chewing. "Today I met a girl out front. She was riding on her bike."

"You went outside?" Mrs. Calloway asked.

"Uh-huh, when you were in back with the telephone man. The girl wants to come visit me tomorrow for a little while. Can she?"

"Of course," Mrs. Calloway told her.

"She's really nice, too. She's really, really nice . . . except—except she's got a skin problem, I guess."

Mr. Calloway asked, "What kind of skin problem?"

"Like maybe some kind of thing where it itches and can't be in the sun very much. She was wearing sunglasses and gloves and boots and a scarf, but—but she's my age. She says she doesn't have any friends either."

"Well," Mr. Calloway declared, "that's sad for her but lucky for you." He raised his eyebrows at his daughter. "Even better, I called around today and found space for you in a softball camp up in Vermont. What do you think of that? Five weeks of ball and swimming. It sounded so perfect to me that I sent them some money to reserve a spot for you." Above them the ceiling beams seemed to groan.

Catie sat back. "But I don't like sports so much, and how 'bout the girl I just met? Mom said if I got a friend I wouldn't have to go away."

"I said *maybe,*" Mrs. Calloway clarified.

Concerned about the ceiling, Mr. Calloway looked upward. "I absolutely think camp would be good for you. I do."

Catie took a deep breath. "But Dad, camp scares me. On television, a camper got dragged away by a grizzly bear. Also, I heard a story where a boy cut off his finger and it fell into the food so that somebody found it." Catie's mouth quivered. "Dad, I don't like camp, especially for five hundred weeks, and I have a friend now. She's my age and everything."

"Catie, I mailed off a deposit," he said. The light above the table dimmed.

"Do you hate me or something?"

Looking at the chandelier, Mr. Calloway said, "Of course not."

"Then why are you making me go?"

"Catie, stop."

"I don't want to leave!"

Mrs. Calloway cleared her throat. She put a hand on her daughter's shoulder. "Clifford, why don't we see how she gets along with this girl tomorrow? Why don't we see?"

Mr. Calloway took a sip of water. He held the glass beside his mouth before placing it down slowly. He leveled his fork at his daughter. "I'm not promising anything," he told her.

Catie broke into a huge smile. She sniffed and said, "We can see! Good. That's so good, because she's lonely like me and wants to be friends, partway because . . . Did I tell you, she can't talk?"

Mrs. Calloway nearly dropped her wineglass. "She can't talk? Then how did she say she wants to come over?"

"She wrote it on a piece of paper."

Mr. Calloway bent forward. "Well, did she write her name, too?"

"Um, yeah."

"So?"

"It's . . . ah . . . It's Allison . . . ah . . . Wondert . . . land."

Mr. Calloway sat back. "Like the story character?"

"I think it's a little different, but I can't remember for sure. Maybe that's her middle name because she reminded her parents of Alice, except she doesn't have yellow hair. Instead, she's almost kinda bald."

"Bald?"

"Yeah. She's almost kinda. It might be because of her skin problem."

Catie was so excited and nervous about her plan that she woke up early the next morning. She went downstairs and sat with her parents in the kitchen. "Allison's so nice," she promised them. After Mr. Calloway left for his office, Catie and Mrs. Calloway waited out on the front porch for Allison Wonderland. By ten, the girl hadn't arrived, so Mrs. Calloway decided to start an exercise video in the den. "Let me know when she's here," she told Catie.

At once, Catie ran upstairs and got out the makeup, clothes, and paint.

"We have to hurry," she told Josephine, who was sitting in a chair beside the dollhouse.

"Okay," Josephine replied and licked her lips nervously.

Catie soaked cotton balls with makeup and mashed them all over her friend's neck and face. She tried to cover every spot and even rubbed some into her hair in case a little showed from under the bandana she was going to wear on her head.

After a few minutes, Josephine asked, "How do I look?"

Catie stepped back. "A little funny. But I told them you've got a skin problem." She applied makeup over Josephine's eyelids. "We'll have to paint your mouth now."

Josephine opened wide and Catie splashed a paintbrush on her tongue. "Can you taste it?"

"No."

Catie scrunched up her face. "It's really red."

"I can say I just had some candy?"

"Maybe just say it's because of everything that's wrong with you."

Catie plunged a new paintbrush in a container of white paint and swabbed it across her friend's teeth and gums. "Oh, that's pretty gross," she said.

"Gross?"

"Like you look bad. Your gums look bad. Don't smile too wide."

Josephine stood up and stared in the mirror. "I believe I look ill, Catie."

"They already know you're not normal. It's okay."

Uncertain, Josephine started dressing. She covered her head in Catie's father's orange bandana and hid her neck in a scarf. She took off her dress and put on a long-sleeved shirt with a picture of a dog on the back. She tucked an old pair of blue jeans into the top of some purple snow boots and pulled on wool gloves.

Catie handed her a pad of paper. "This is for writing things." Catie stood back and smiled.

Josephine said, "What if your mother looks at me hard?"

"It's okay. Mom doesn't look at things that way, especially things that are hard to look at . . . like you."

Josephine rang the front doorbell.

Catie, who had just secretly let her out, let her back in. "Hey, Allison," she said loudly, like she hadn't seen the girl since the day before.

Josephine wrote, *Hello, Catie.*

Having heard the doorbell, Mrs. Calloway came in from the den. Reaching the foyer, she stopped short.

Catie said, "Mom, Allison's here to play."

Mrs. Calloway looked away from the girl's blotchy face. She walked closer and held her breath. "Nice to meet you, Allison."

Josephine adjusted her sunglasses and wrote, *Thank you. Nice to meet you, ma'am.* She lifted up the pad to show what she'd written.

Mrs. Calloway nodded. "So you live around here?"

Josephine wrote, *Yes, ma'am, right around here.*

"It certainly seems like a wonderful neighborhood."

It's good, ma'am.

Mrs. Calloway studied the wool gloves Josephine had on. "So, ah, Catie told us you have a medical condition."

Yes, ma'am. I'm ugly and have bad skin and teeth.

Mrs. Calloway struggled to smile. "Oh, you'll prob . . . well, maybe, grow out of it. Who knows? The thing I always tell Catie is that beauty is on the inside."

Yes, ma'am, Josephine wrote.

Peering into the girl's face, Mrs. Calloway flinched. Swallowing, she asked, "Will—will you have lunch with us?"

Josephine lifted the pad and scrawled, *No, thank you, ma'am. I am reckwired to dine on special food.*

Catie explained to her mother, "They grind up Allison's sandwiches because she can only eat with a spoon."

Mrs. Calloway dropped her gaze, which landed on the girl's boots and pants. She hesitated.

Catie jerked her mother's sleeve. "Allison's got boots and pants like mine, but they're different."

At that, Josephine's lipstick-smeared mouth stretched into a tense smile, exposing reddish pink teeth and gums.

Mrs. Calloway turned away. She gathered herself and walked over to the couch to fluff a pillow. "Catie, what—what do you and Allison plan to do this morning?"

"Go play in my room. She likes Barbies and dollhouses."

"Well, have fun," Mrs. Calloway said, biting her bottom lip.

As soon as her mother and father sat down for dinner, Catie said, "Mom, tell Dad how Allison is."

Mrs. Calloway's eyes shifted toward her husband. "She was sweet."

Catie said, "She was cool, too."

"She seemed like a good girl." Mrs. Calloway took a sip of water. "But Catie, I hope you know that she's a very sick girl. Do you?"

"Not so sick she isn't funner than everybody."

"But she is very sick. You do realize that? I don't know what she has, but she could be . . . I wouldn't be shocked to find out that she's very, very ill."

Catie sat up. "I know she's not dying."

Mr. Calloway explained, "Sweetheart, nobody's saying that."

"Good, because she's fine."

He said, "But it does happen. I'm sorry to say it, but children do sometimes die."

Catie shrank back in her chair. "Well, I know she's not because she wants to be my permanent friend. She hasn't had a friend as good as me for her whole life. Until we met, we were the loneliest people in the world."

Mr. Calloway touched a hand to one of his daughter's. "Don't say that, Catieboo."

"It's true, and if you send me away, it'll get worse even. Why do I have to leave and go to camp when I only wanna stay? I've got someone to play with, and I'm sick of feeling dumb and unliked in new places."

Mr. Calloway winced. "Catie, have you ever considered that Allison might very well be going away this summer? She might have camps to attend or things to do with her own family. We don't know."

A tear wandered down Catie's narrow face. "Allison isn't going anywhere. She's staying because she feels happy I'm her friend."

Mr. Calloway froze for a second, then he said, "She told you that?"

"Yeah."

He adjusted his shirt collar. "Don't cry."

"Why not?"

"Because it makes me feel crummy. Because I want you to be a happy girl. I know we move too much. I know that. I know you must feel uprooted constantly, and I want you to feel connected."

"I'm connected up with my new friend."

"What if it turns out, after a few weeks, that you two don't get along?"

"We will. I know we will."

Mrs. Calloway said, "Clifford, don't torture her. What's your decision?"

It took him a moment, then he said, "No camp. I've decided no camp."

Upstairs there was an enormous thump, as if something or someone had jumped for joy.

16

In bed, Catie listened to the cicadas calling in the trees. She smiled to herself and squeezed Red Dog. Her dad was going to let her stay at home all summer. She was so relieved that she couldn't fall asleep. Across the room, her door slowly swung open.

In the darkness, Josephine glowed brilliantly, her crow friend on her shoulder as if she were a pirate princess.

Catie scooted out from beneath her sheets. "Josephine, did you hear what my dad said?"

"Yes," she answered, smiling broadly.

Unable to contain herself, Catie rushed over and hugged Josephine. "We can be best friends now."

Josephine smiled widely. "Mr. Crow said we need to have a celebration party! We could have a tea party."

Catie's eyes grew large and curious. "Up in the attic?"

Josephine turned. "I've got a better idea." Closing her eyes, she raised her hands toward the ceiling, and the middles of her palms glowed. Mr. Crow glided off her shoulder, landing alongside the plastic front porch of the dollhouse. Then there was a brush of wind, and Catie and Josephine were standing in the dollhouse.

"Oh, my gosh!" Catie said.

"Isn't this wonderful?"

"It's even cooler than when I went to Disneyland."

Josephine smiled and took Catie's hand. She led her up the steps to the second floor, where Catie sat down on some brightly colored plastic furniture near a small table with a fancy silver tea set on top. "I guess we can't really eat things."

"No."

Catie squinted. "You know what? You sorta look like a doll."

"You and I both. It's so we're just right for playing in a dollhouse."

Catie shook her head. "Um, you wanna make a toast?"

Josephine lifted her teacup. "We need to say something beautiful."

Catie said, "To Catie and Josephine. Is that okay?"

Josephine smiled. "And Allison Wondertland."

"Yeah, her also."

So Catie and Josephine, looking like dolls, tapped their cups together and pretended to drink.

In the weeks that followed, the girls played together as much as possible, up in the attic, in Catie's room, and out in the backyard. To keep Mr. and Mrs. Calloway satisfied, Josephine visited regularly as Allison Wondertland. Mostly, though, she came secretly as herself, invisible to Catie's parents but perfectly visible to Catie. Soon enough, the loneliness that had gripped Catie's and Josephine's very different worlds fell away like the details of ancient memories. In fact, every room in the house reflected their growing happiness, while outside, the flowers bloomed so large and bright that Mrs. Calloway had to wear sunglasses when she worked in the garden.

Most of the time, Catie and Josephine had been careful to keep their activities hidden. Whenever they did anything together, they listened intently for Catie's parents' footsteps, and if they played out in the yard, Catie took a moment to invent a good fib as to why she was running around by herself or jabbering to herself in the warm air. However, their friendship quickly grew so comfortable and their time together so ordinary that they both, inevitably, became careless.

On a Saturday in July, Mr. Calloway passed by his daughter's room. He stopped and watched as Catie, who was resting on the floor, played with a Barbie. Then he saw something impossible and rubbed his eyes. When he refocused them, a second Barbie continued moving around his daughter as if guided by unseen hands. "Catie?" Mr. Calloway said.

The hovering Barbie toppled over, and Catie whirled about. "Dad?"

"Catie, that doll. Was it floating?"

She glanced from him to Bride Barbie and back. "I—I don't think so."

"It was. I saw it." Mr. Calloway stepped into her room.

Catie swallowed and studied the spot where Josephine had just vanished. "It wasn't."

He crossed the carpet, leaned down, and picked up Bride Barbie. "Catie, I saw it moving."

"Maybe I was holding her feet."

He stood quietly.

"Dad, I was holding her feet, like she was walking."

Mr. Calloway didn't speak. He stared at the wall and appeared to consider the possibilities. Finally, he said, "I guess I didn't see your hand."

When her father was gone, Catie lowered her head to the rug and breathed in deeply. She told herself that she would pay better attention to where her parents were in the house. Even with her best efforts, though, they had another close call.

On a rainy, thundery morning, when Allison was finished visiting, Mrs. Calloway put on a raincoat and insisted on driving her home.

Frantic, Catie said, "That's not a very nice thing to offer."

"It's pouring out," Mrs. Calloway told her daughter.

My house isn't so good, Josephine quickly wrote.

"That's okay."

She scribbled, *My parents would get upset if I brought you to see it.*

Mrs. Calloway looked into Allison's sunglasses. She flinched when she

caught sight of the girl's teeth. "Allison, is there something I should know?"

Catie grabbed one of her mother's sleeves. "Mom, stop, okay? They're poor and embarrassed that their house is bad."

Josephine wrote, *My home's got a big problem. We've got mean, escaped chikens walking around the yard.*

"Chickens?" Mrs. Calloway asked.

and a giant dog.

Mrs. Calloway took a deep breath.

Josephine wrote, *Thank you, ma'am,* and was out the door.

Somehow, though, neither the floating doll or Allison's escaped "chikens" caused Mr. or Mrs. Calloway to pay closer attention to the details of their daughter's happy life, and Catie and Josephine's magical summer continued unbroken.

One lazy afternoon, as Mrs. Calloway worked in the backyard, the two girls sat together like old friends in the kitchen. Josephine was invisible and made sure not to pick up anything for fear that Mrs. Calloway might walk in. Meanwhile, Catie ate a snack and quietly asked Josephine questions. "Josephine, does it make you sad that you can't ever have sweets again?"

Josephine squinched her mouth. "Not so much. I forgot what they taste like."

"They're good." Catie ate another cookie. "Does it make you sad you can't ever go swimming again?"

"I never went swimming when I was alive."

"Oh." Catie drank some milk, surprised that Josephine had never been in a pool. She asked, "What were things like when you were little?"

"I don't know. They were just different."

"Like how?" Catie folded her arms on the kitchen table and rested her chin on a wrist. "Can you show me?"

Josephine raised her eyebrows. In an instant, the flat light fixture on the ceiling changed into a big, heavy, old-fashioned light. Then, as if a gentle wave had rippled across the room, the kitchen became old-timey.

Catie lifted her head. She asked, "This is how the kitchen was?"

"Yes."

She got up and poked around the nearly empty room. "Oh, my gosh. Is that skinny thing your stove?"

"It's the one my mom used."

"It looks like a metal box with legs." Catie turned and walked across the wooden floor, stopping by the enormous white sink. "I guess you guys didn't own much, did you?"

Josephine drifted behind her. "There weren't so many things in a kitchen back then."

"Where's your toaster and coffee maker and microwave?"

"They weren't invented yet."

"Well, how'd you cook?"

"Do you want to see?"

"If you can show me, yeah."

At that, an old-fashioned lady came into the room. Her shoes were hard and pointy and clopped loudly on the floor. She wore a fluffy white blouse and a long white skirt. Her hair was pulled back into a large bun. The lady reached into the deep sink and picked out a few peeled potatoes. She turned and took a pot from a steel rack on the wall, filled it with water, then banged it down on the stove. She paused a moment before dropping the potatoes in and striking a big wooden match to light the burner.

Catie glanced at her friend. "Josephine," she said, "is that your mom?"

"Yes."

Catie watched the lady, who was strong and short and not so beautiful,

collect the potato peelings from the sink. "Now I know why your clothes are funny."

Josephine smiled at Catie's comment. As her mother began making bread, the scene rippled and vanished.

Catie said, "Will you let me see her again? And your dad?"

"Probably sometime."

They sat down and were quiet for a few minutes. Finally, Catie asked, "Was everything different?"

"It was."

"It must be hard, the way things have changed?"

"It is."

Catie looked at the table. "Well, do you want to go up to my room and draw pictures of the past? I can draw how it was back when I was a kid, and you can draw how it was when you were."

The next morning, while Mrs. Calloway paid the bills, Catie played with Josephine up in her room. Excited, she grabbed up Fashion Barbie and explained that the doll was an undercover police officer arresting bank robbers and diamond thieves. At that, Josephine took hold of Bride Barbie and said she was a famous nurse in France whose sweet personality had saved a hundred injured soldiers.

Catie whispered, "How'd the soldiers get hurt?"

"In the war my dad went to."

"Where was it?"

"Way over in Europe."

"Oh, it was across the ocean." Catie stayed quiet for a minute before saying, "I really liked that old stuff you showed me yesterday. You think you can show me more?"

Josephine looked away. "Sometimes seeing the past makes me a little sad. I miss it. Maybe I can show you something else, like . . . like a circus or something?"

"A circus!" Catie exclaimed. "That's perfect."

Josephine took a moment to relax. She smiled, and when she waved her hand, a top hat appeared. She showed Catie that it was empty, turned away, and pulled out a white rabbit.

"He's so cute," Catie whispered.

Josephine put the rabbit down on the floor, where it hopped about quietly. She raised her arms, and a shower of flower petals began falling from the ceiling.

Catie stood up and let them land against her face. "I can feel them," she said in a hushed voice.

A flaming ring suddenly appeared in one of Josephine's hands, and without warning a lion sprang out of Catie's closet, leaped through the ring, and turned into a tiny French poodle on the other side.

Catie's mouth went slack.

Josephine pointed. "Go look outside your door."

Catie did, and saw that an elephant was standing in the hallway eating peanuts. She touched one of its legs and stared at it for a few minutes. Swelling with appreciation, she turned and smiled at Josephine.

Josephine smiled back and said, "You wanted to see a circus."

Catie spun about. "Now I have to show you something cool, it's only fair." She glanced around for a second, then went to her desk and flicked on the radio. She turned up the volume and yelled, "Oh, yeah! Oh, yeah, baby! We got an elephant in the hall and my mom can't hear us now!" She looked at Josephine. "I want to teach you how to dance!"

"No thank you."

"Come on! It's easy."

Josephine said, "I'm not good at that kind of thing," and the circus animals faded away.

"That's why I'm showing you," Catie told her, bouncing her hips and shoulders back and forth. "Just move around to the music."

Josephine moved a little.

"See!" Catie told her. "You're a pop star. Go, 'Yeah, yeah, yeah!'"

Josephine moved a little more.

"Now go, 'Yeah, yeah, yeah!'"

"Yeah, yeah, yeah!" Josephine said stiffly.

After dancing for a while, Catie turned down the radio and collapsed on her bed. With her face smashed into Red Dog, she said, "I knew you could play like a pop star."

Josephine said, "I didn't do such a good job."

"Yes, you did." Catie rested for a second before her mouth popped open. "I've got an idea." Bouncing to her feet, she rushed to her closet and rustled through a box. "Let's take a picture of us."

"What if I'm invisible?"

"But Josephine, film isn't a grownup, it's film. It maybe can see you." Catie found her camera and hurried over to her desk. "All I have to do is set the timer so we can be in the picture together." Catie aimed the camera toward Josephine. She turned a knob and pushed a button before rushing to her friend. "Make a pretty face," she said, and waved. The camera flashed, and soon a picture started to spit out the front. The two girls hurried to look.

"That's the photograph coming out?" Josephine asked.

"Yup," Catie said as, slowly, the two of them began to appear.

Later that afternoon Mr. Calloway arrived home from work early.

Catie and Mrs. Calloway were emptying the last few boxes in Catie's room.

Mr. Calloway came up the steps slowly. He stopped at the top, turned, and walked through his daughter's doorway.

When Mrs. Calloway saw his face, she asked, "Are you feeling okay?"

Mr. Calloway yanked off his tie and draped it over one of his daughter's chairs. "I'm a bad guy. That's how I feel."

"Why do you say that?"

He stared at the floor, then at his wife. "I wish things were different."

Mrs. Calloway said, "Nothing has to be. Everything's fine."

"No, everything's not."

"What is it?"

He tightened his lips and said, "I'm getting transferred. We have to move again . . . soon."

Mrs. Calloway staggered backward. She put a hand on her stomach as if she might be sick.

Catie's head jerked around. "What?"

Mr. Calloway hesitated before speaking. "Catie, sweetheart, we've got to move. I—I was told this afternoon."

The room seemed to shudder and fade to a brown-gray color.

"But we can't!" Catie said.

"We have to," he told her. "I'm sorry."

Catie studied his face and began crying. "But, Dad, I won't leave for anything!"

"I understand," he said softly. "I know you don't want to."

21

The house felt overwhelmed by lonely shadows. Amid them, Mr. and Mrs. Calloway endured their disappointment. But that night Catie cried into her dinner, over her dessert, and for hours on the couch in the dark living room. In fact, she wept for two straight days. Outside, rain beat down and thunder rumbled. As for Josephine, she was nowhere to be found.

On the third day, when the sun finally shone again, Catie went outside and sulked all morning at the picnic table on the back porch.

Worried, Mrs. Calloway phoned her husband. During his lunch hour, he came home and sat down beside his daughter. After a minute, he said, "It's a nice view from here, huh?"

"I don't like it anymore."

He put an arm around her. "Oh, Catie, it'll always be a nice view. If you let it sit in your memory, it will always be beautiful."

A tear jittered from one of Catie's eyes and curled around her jaw. "This was the best place for me. I had a friend, and I liked our house."

Mr. Calloway hunched his shoulders. "I know, and I'm so, so sorry. It hurts me to see you so sad."

Catie leaned forward and started crying, softly at first, then so hard that her body shook and her voice came out between sobs. "What am I gonna do without Allison? I . . . love her so much. What will I do all alone in a new place?"

Mr. Calloway pulled his daughter to him. "If I could give you happiness, I would do it, Catieboo. Your mother and I worry that we've put you through too much. Please, sweetie, tell me you're okay."

"I'm not," Catie told him.

"You are. You've got us. You've got us, and we would bend over backward for you."

Catie continued whimpering.

Mr. Calloway lifted a hand to a flat spot just below one of her eyes. He touched it softly, then showed her the eyelash on the tip of his finger. "Make a wish," he said, "and blow the lash away, and it might come true."

Straight away, Catie blew it off his finger. She said, "I wish I could take Allison with me."

"I wish you could, too. I wish you could, too."

22

Nearly a week went by, and Josephine hadn't appeared. Every day Catie pleaded with the empty air. "Please, come talk to me," but Josephine didn't.

Eventually, Mrs. Calloway asked Catie why Allison Wondertland hadn't been around.

"I guess she's mad we're leaving," Catie answered.

The following day, Catie grew so furious with Josephine that she stamped out to the backyard and sat down in the grass. She pulled her knees to her chest and looked high up at the attic window. She whispered, "You're a liar. You said you were my best friend, but if you were, you'd come out."

Nothing.

"Josephine, you're a liar," she repeated. She closed her eyes. "Liar. Liar. Liar. Liar," she said over and over and over.

Long minutes went by, then a scratchy voice answered, "I am not."

Catie's eyes cracked open. "You are."

"You're the one who's leaving."

"It's not my fault."

Josephine's mouth wiggled sadly.

"Come with me," Catie said.

"I can't."

"Try."

"But . . . I can't! That's all!"

Catie swept a hand through the grass. "You said you couldn't dance, either, but you can."

Upset, Josephine crossed her legs and floated in the air. "Mr. Crow

says another kid might move in. That's what he says. That's what I hope for."

Catie glared at her. "Either way, I have to go off by myself, and I hate it. I hate leaving and being new, and I especially hate how you don't care."

Josephine glared back. "At least you have your parents to be with. I don't have mine anymore."

At that, Catie's anger drained away. "Josephine," she said faintly, "a new kid won't love you as much as me. No one can."

"I . . . know."

"I'll miss you a thousand percent. I already do."

Josephine sniffled.

"But I'll be your friend forever, even when I'm far away. I *will* be."

Josephine nodded.

Two more weeks went by, and Mr. Calloway's suitcases were packed. One morning he hugged his wife and daughter and flew away to Buffalo, New York. Day after gloomy day passed, and Catie and Josephine sat beside each other for hours, rarely making a sound and barely moving. The loneliness that had so recently vanished from their lives returned.

One morning, some people from the moving company came and packed all of the Calloways' belongings. Catie and Josephine watched as a round lady lowered the dollhouse into a large brown box. Before she could drop Bride Barbie in, Catie gave her to Josephine.

Josephine smiled. "I wish I had something to give you."

Catie said, "I have our picture together."

A day later, a moving van pulled up out front. Catie went looking for

Josephine. "We're going in a few hours," she called into the empty attic. "I don't have a plan to save us. I tried to think of one a hundred times, but I couldn't."

There was no answer.

She looked around and saw Mr. Crow standing in the open attic window.

"Hey, Mr. Crow," Catie said.

He let out a weak squawk and flew away over the yard.

Catie wandered to the window and watched him circle down to the ground, landing beside Josephine, who stood in the grass.

Josephine waved.

Catie waved back and wished for the middle of the summer again, when they hadn't known she was going to leave.

Josephine waved again.

Catie did the same. She blinked and looked at the iron fence and the old garage. She scanned their big tree and the garden. Her eyes moved back to Josephine.

Josephine waved once more.

Catie stared at her. She squinted and measured distances with her eyes. Her mouth opened, and she yelled, "Josephine, you can do it!" Spinning about, she raced from the window and pounded down the stairs, her legs feeling weak and wobbly.

In the kitchen, her mother asked, "Where are you going?"

Catie called, "Outside!" She flung open the door to the porch and ran out and down the steps. At the bottom, she stopped and stared at her friend. "You're out of our yard," she said softly.

Josephine floated a few inches above the neighbor's property.

"I know."

"You said you couldn't leave."

"I did tell you that, and . . . I never have. It's been so long. I don't want to lie to you about it anymore, though. I can leave, but I'm scared to. This is where my parents and my sisters lived. I was born here. It's the only thing I know about."

"Josephine, you think you might come with me?"

"I—I don't want to be lonely."

Catie shook her head. A smile flashed across her lips. "Josephine, I'll always be your friend. I'll stay with you forever, and when I get too old to see you, we'll put you in clothes like Allison."

Josephine added, "I don't want *you* to be lonely either."

"I won't be," Catie said.

Models:
Catie . . . Claudia Buccino
Josephine . . . Carlene Buccino

We would like to thank the following people and organizations for their help. First, our families deserve enormous credit for their support and encouragement. Without them, this book would not exist in any form. Of course, we thank Claudia and Carlene, who were amazingly adept and natural throughout the photo shoots. We sincerely appreciate Cory, who was a wonderful help when it came to managing the stars, props, and crow wrangling. Thanks to Dan for being a good father in the story and out. Kathryn Parke was an adept and resourceful seamstress for costumes. Extra special thanks to Angela Talbot, whose amazing dolls, both animal and human, gave the book an extra measure of joy. And thanks to Susan Mangan, whose typographical finesse unifies the illustration and the story.

Of course we are unbelievably indebted to Eden Edwards, Bob Kosturko, and Houghton Mifflin for their trust and vision. And none of this would have been possible without the dedication of Robbie Hare, our matchless literary agent.

Thanks to Fuji for use of a digital FinePix S2 Pro to photograph the images in this book. Thanks to Adobe for helping fantasy to become reality. All models were photographed in a studio and digitally composited into separately photographed and created backgrounds using Adobe Photoshop 7. Thanks to Dragon Wing Studios for the crow costume.